Diary of a Christmas Wombat

written by

Jackie French

illustrated by

Bruce Whatley

HarperCollins *Children's Books*

First published in hardback in Australia by HarperCollins Publishers Pty Limited in 2011
First published in paperback in Great Britain by HarperCollins Children's Books in 2012

10 9 8 7 6 5 4 3 2 1

ISBN: 978-0-00-749071-4

HarperCollins Children's Books is a division of HarperCollins Publishers Ltd.
The author and illustrator assert the moral right to be identified as the author and illustrator of the work.
A CIP catalogue record for this title is available from the British Library.

Visit our website at: www.harpercollins.co.uk

Bruce Whatley used acrylic paints on watercolour paper to create the illustrations in this book
Original cover and internal design by Priscilla Neilsen; based on a design by HarperCollins Design Studio

Printed and bound in China

To Beth, with love and wombats.
JF

For Lana, Lincoln and Harry – Merry Christmas.
BW

Slept.

Scratched.

Slept.

Ate grass.

Dangly things bumped against my nose!

Got rid of them.

Smelled **carrots**!

Strange creatures are eating my carrots!

Fought major battle
with strange creatures!

Won the battle.

Feeling tired.

Found the perfect spot
to have a nap.

ZZZZZZZZZ

I smell carrots!

Strange creatures trying
to eat my carrots!

Got rid of them.

Again.

Carrots delicious.

Off to find MORE carrots.

A wombat hole?

Carrots!

Not easy to
get back up.

Scratched.

Have misjudged
strange creatures.
They can be useful
for finding carrots.

Never knew there were so many carrots in the world!

Carrots!

Carrots!

My carrots!

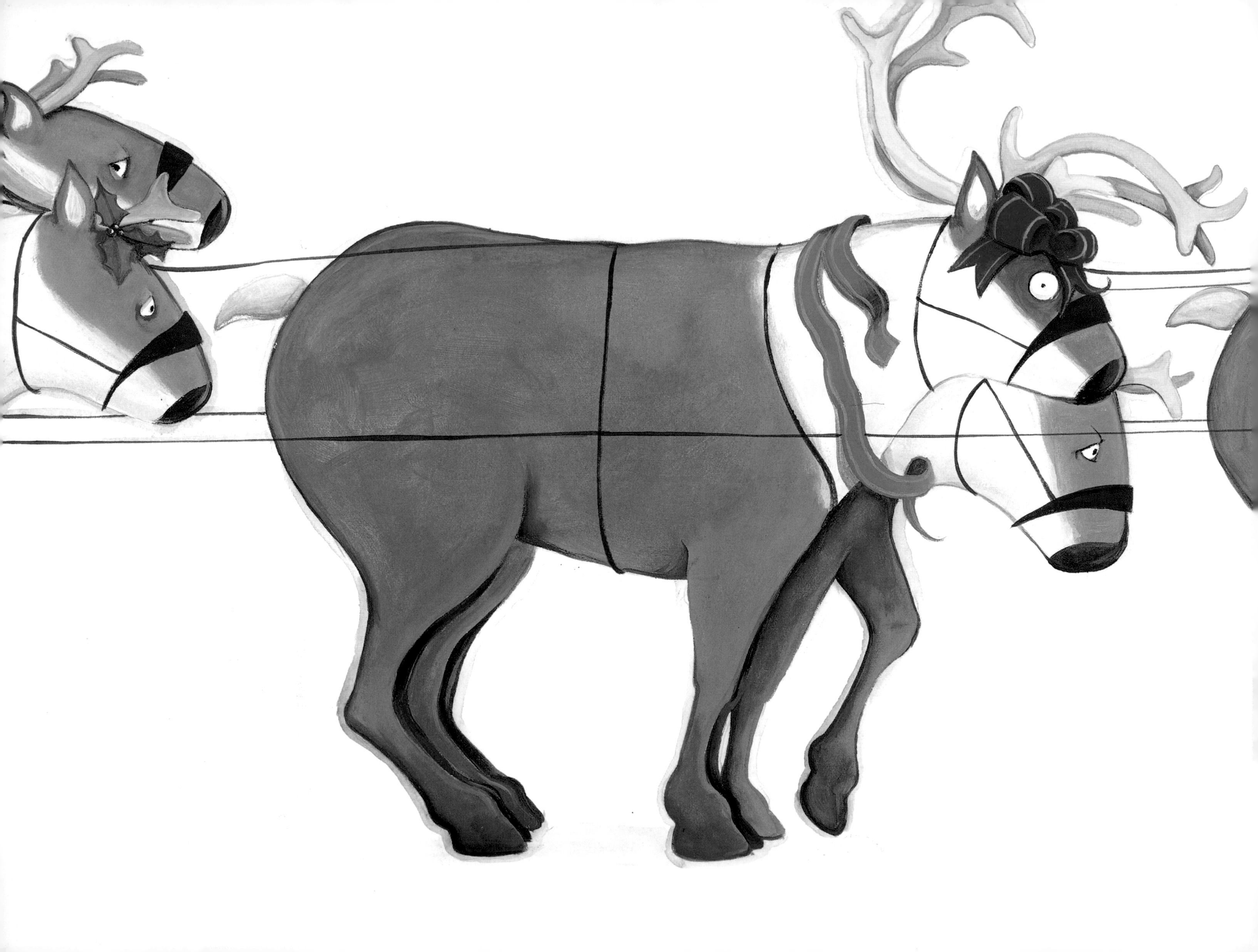

Said goodbye to
strange creatures.
Hope they visit
again soon!

Grass delicious... but for some reason not hungry.

Slept.